The Linemen's Game

HARLEY LEE JAMES

authorHOUSE®

AuthorHouse™
1663 Liberty Drive
Bloomington, IN 47403
www.authorhouse.com
Phone: 833-262-8899

Published by AuthorHouse 01/14/2022

ISBN: 978-1-6655-4689-8 (sc)
ISBN: 978-1-6655-4687-4 (hc)
ISBN: 978-1-6655-4688-1 (e)

Library of Congress Control Number: 2021924839

H E CAME INTO my life like a shooting star; sudden and shining brightly. The light of a shooting star eventually burns out but an impression to those who saw it always remains. Why do we leave many stones unturned? The answer is fear. We like to be comfortable, therefore we long to be in stable and unchanging situations. Many people never achieve their dreams because they stop chasing them. The constant changing situations that we encounter on the path to our dream drives many of us away. Stability and consistency are more comfortable than living day to day.

I was nineteen years old when my parents died in a plane crash. My father was the CEO of Summer Enterprises. Every summer I sat in meetings with my dad, taking notes as I watched him secure project after project.

I was not the typical beautiful woman. I did not wear a size two. I was not afraid to work for what I wanted. I did not need hours to paint my face on in the mornings. If someone did not like the way I looked I viewed that as their problem, not mine. I most certainly was not the woman asked out on dates. I was enthusiastic about my job. Protecting people was my passion. Every day I stepped onto the road with confidence.

I had no idea why he chose me to fixate on? Pretty and beautiful were words I usually heard when a man wanted to get in my pants. He was different. He had his sight on me from day one and I have no idea why.

CHAPTER 1

IT WAS MY tenth year running the business when I decided to open a traffic control division. The new division opened in the winter and employee after employee resigned. It was late spring when I decided it was time for a change. I was going under cover to find out what was making our flaggers so unhappy.

It was my first day on the job when I met Lee. The morning had started out troublesome. Just as I got to the location the truck began to overheat. Felicia, one of my coworkers, pulled the radiator cap off and anti-freeze bubbled everywhere. Worst part was she lost the cap when she pulled it off. I was working on the truck when I felt like someone was watching me. I looked over towards the crew and noticed a man I had never seen before. He leaned against an HJL truck facing me. At first, he seemed to be watching traffic in the intersection. When I turned back a second time, I noticed him turning his head.

I walked over to get a closer look. As I got closer, I noticed a rugged country boy appearance. I passed him and started a conversation with Red. Red was an apprentice around my age. He towered over most of the guys on the crew except the guy leaning against the truck. I was about to mingle into the group when I heard Felicia's voice. "Are you married?"

"I'm divorced," said the tall man with a thick southern accent. I turned and walked to the tailgate of the truck, conveniently placing myself between Felicia and the man.

"Where is your accent from," asked Felicia.

"Georgia." As he said this Mark gave the cut signal. I walked over to the truck and poured eight bottles of water into the reservoir. This did not even touch the surface. I grabbed my wallet and approached Mark.

"Can you take me to get anti-freeze?"

"I can't but Daniel can." He leaned out the window and called to Daniel, "Can you take her. I would but I got a long drive."

"Yes." I climbed in the passenger seat of Daniel's company truck. He was still writing notes on a book he had balanced on his steering wheel. The tall man approached his window.

"Where are you going, Danny," he asked with an implying tone.

"To the auto parts store. Her truck overheated," he said without looking up from his writing.

"I can take her. You can go home."

"I don't have as long of a drive home as you do, I will take her."

"I don't mind. I don't have any plans."

This time Daniel looked up from his book and stated firmly, "I will take her." He put his seatbelt on and grabbed the shifter. We drove off leaving the man standing there watching us disappear.

This was my first encounter with Lee. "Why did you have to steal my spotlight?"

"Felicia, what are you talking about?"

"He was talking to me. He wouldn't want someone like you anyway." I ignored her and kept driving. She was right though, guys like Lee usually did not go for women like me. I was not ugly, nor did I view myself that way either, but the unspoken rule of society was that men with good paying jobs went for women who wore a size two at max, painted their faces on daily, and did not hold jobs that required physical labor.

The next day I approached Mark and he pointed towards Lee. I turned to Lee, "What's the plan?"

"You always approach me with such authority." I looked at him dumbfounded as to what to say. "I always feel like I'm going to get in trouble when you come here."

I blushed and looked back towards Mark. He was still on the phone. Lee walked over to his truck and Greg approached me. "When he comes back tell him he's fired."

"What?"

"Just do it." He was smiling in an ever so creepy way. Lee walked back with a blueprint in his hands.

"Lee, you're fired!" His head dropped, like a sad puppy. He walked back to his truck. Mark looked in the rear-view mirror and got out of his truck as he noticed Lee walking away.

"Did he tell you where we are working yet?"

"No, the young lady here just gave the man a tough time," said Greg still dawning that crooked smile.

"Just set up like yesterday, please," Mark said as he rushed back to his truck phone still in hand.

Later that day I was sitting in the truck watching the HJL crew work. Lee had been working not too far away from me when Kayla walked up to the window. "How are you today?"

"Fine thanks just drinking some water to cool down." I grabbed a bottle of water and looked away from Lee. I could not keep my eyes off Lee. He bent over to pick something up and my heart jumped. Kayla looked over at Lee and back to me, then started fanning me with a clip board she had in her hand. "What are you doing?"

"Cooling you down."

"Sorry, the heat is bothering me today."

"Lee is bothering you today."

"What, no! That's ridiculous."

"He likes you. It's obvious."

"You really think so?"

"I know so."

CHAPTER 2

THE FOLLOWING WEEK I got assigned to the Newberry Hill project. I arrived onsite early and noticed two HJL trucks already there. I jumped out and walked up to the bucket truck. The man inside the truck said, "The foreman will be here soon." As I walked away, he called out the window, "Young lady?"

"Yes, he wants to set up the whole span. On second thought you just wait for him to get here." Once again, I headed back towards the truck and this time an HJL pickup truck pulled up.

"While on my jobsite you shall wear proper work attire," he said in a firm, demanding tone.

"Sorry, I was just getting." I noticed that my explanation was not amusing him and rushed back to get my boots. I grabbed my boots and put them on. "Harry, we better be on our game today."

"Why?"

"The boss isn't too happy. Gave me a lecture about my flip flops this morning. I hustled back towards the truck but got stopped by the same lineman I spoke with earlier.

He held up a video on his phone and said, "Look at those gigantic hands holding that tiny bird. Have you ever met Henry?"

"No." Lee had pulled up, so he was behind me.

"Open the door and look." I pulled on the door handle. Lee looked up from his book and unlocked the door. I opened the door and there sat a bird cage containing a black bird. He had toys, treats, food, and water. "I wanted to snap his neck, but Lee wouldn't let me."

I was glad that Lee had not allowed his crew to kill Henry. The guy from the passenger seat was now standing by the front of the truck. "Look at those gigantic hands feeding that bird."

"That's not the only thing that's big. Everything on Lee is huge and I mean everything." His emphasis on the word everything angered me.

"Just because a man is tall doesn't mean that he's well endowed."

"I can prove it to you. I have a video of Lee taking a leak. The other day he was at his truck taking a leak I video recorded it from the bucket." I turned and looked at Lee expecting him to be angry that his crew invaded his privacy. However, he was still writing on his book. "You know what they say. Take the size of a man's shoe and subtract two."

"I wear a size fourteen boot," said Lee startling me that he was allowing them to talk like this. I turned and looked at him.

I started walking towards the truck when Greg called out, "Lee is our blue-ribbon calf."

I admired the way Lee collaborated with his crew. Rolling up wires, grabbing tools, digging holes, even helping me move the work zone around. I was standing in the middle of the zone watching driveways when I thought someone was watching me. I turned towards Lee and saw him look away quickly. I smiled and walked up the zone to pick up a cone that a driver kept knocking over.

The next morning, I got assigned to a different jobsite. Kayla parked and hurried over to me. "Lee is freaking out. He refuses to set up unless you are there." She took my sign and motioned for me to go. I traveled up the hill, as I passed Lee, he threw me a seductive look. Later that afternoon, once the zone moved Becky and I were standing on the shoulder talking.

"Lee watches your every move like you have complete control over him."

"No, he doesn't."

"Yes, he does." Take a drink of your soda once.

"What?"

"Just do it." I took a sip and watched Lee. As soon as his eye caught my arm movement, he locked eyes on me. At the end of the day Lee approached me.

"I won't see you Friday. I have a class." The way he said class made me want him. Jasper, who had been filing in for Tim interrupted my moment.

"Sarah, maybe Friday after work we can catch a movie?" Lee shot him the dirty looks. He crossed the half circle we were standing in, placing himself closer to me than Jasper.

"Thanks, Jasper but I have plans Friday night."

"You have a date," asked Becky.

"No, a friend is in town, and we are getting dinner."

"So, a date," countered Tim.

"Not a date," I said as I walked to the truck.

"You missed it today, Sarah. Greg ran up behind people with a wet shirt and snapping them in the ass with it. He got to Lee, and he cracked him in the back with the shirt. Lee turned and gave him the dirtiest look. Greg went to the truck for an hour and didn't come out."

"He didn't mention that."

"When did he talk to you?"

"He called me while I was on lunch."

"No wonder he was mad. I would be mad to if someone interrupted my conversation with the woman I was trying to impress."

7

"You guys exaggerate how much I mean to him."

"What would you do with a man like Lee?"

"He would be spoiled. Lunch packed, house cleaned, and dinner on the table every day when he got home."

"Among other things," snickered Tim.

"Obviously."

"Show him you are interested then. Give the man what he wants." The rest of the trip went in silence.

The next morning, I was on my way to Newberry Hill when Lee sent me a message. I was about to reply when my phone rang. "I cannot talk to you if you do not respond to me." My eyes grew big, and my heart raced. "Did you get my message?"

"Yes, I was typing a response when you called."

"We are going on storm duty. I will see you tomorrow."

"Ok, I am almost there. Kayla is coming out so I will go to the meeting spot and sit until she comes. You can sign the paper tomorrow." When I hung up the phone, I fanned myself. "That was hot."

"What did he say?" I recapped the conversation to Becky. "He wanted a reason to hear your voice."

"No way."

"He won't see you today, he needed to hear your voice." I arrived on Newberry Hill and parked.

"Hey guys."

"Hey Kayla." We got out of the truck and were talking when I noticed a tall man standing on the hill watching me. I quickly looked away and drove up the hill.

"I thought you were on storm duty?"

"I am."

"What brings you here?"

"I had to check out a pole. A car hit it but its ok."

"I see," I said slightly disappointed that he was not here for me.

"Sarah, would you like to go on a trip this weekend?"

"Sure. I think I can adjust my schedule."

"I will pick you up Friday after my class is over."

"Sounds good. I better get back before they come looking for me."

CHAPTER 3

FRIDAY AFTERNOON I paced my apartment unsure what to pack. Becky was sitting on my bed helping me chose my clothes. I pulled out my bikini and held it up. "Bold choice."

"It's the only swimsuit I have." Becky threw it in my suitcase before I could reject the idea of taking it. I was almost finished packing when my phone rang.

"Are you almost ready?"

"Yes."

"Good send me your address. Make sure you bring a swimsuit."

"I'm so nervous. I should cancel."

"No," said Becky wrestling the phone from my hands. "You got this. Besides, he's putty in your hands."

"What?"

"Anytime you do anything with your mouth he melts. The other morning when you ate an apple onsite man, he was dying."

"You mean the other day when he was dancing onsite?"

"Yes, that had to be a sexy sight."

"It was. But I do not get it. Why make remarks and not just talk to me?"

"The idea of you naked probably makes him nervous. He seems like the type to take things slow."

"A true southern gentleman." I opened it to see Lee standing there with a dozen peach roses. "Thank-you," I said admiring the roses. "Would you like to come in?"

"No, are you ready?"

"Yes," said Becky as she took the roses from my hand and placed my suitcase beside me. "I will put these in water for you. Have fun." I walked outside and Lee took my bag. We got on the highway and drove for what seemed like ages.

"Where are we going?"

"My cabin on the Flint River." We arrived at the cabin late that evening. He led me to the grand master bedroom. Stone covered the walls, a waterfall led way to a swimming pool, through the doors I could see a hot tub near the master bathroom.

"This is beautiful."

"Nothing compares to my view from here," he said handing me a fluffy towel. He slid my shirt up over my head. My body tingled at his touch. He took his shirt off and tossed it to the floor. His bare chest against mine. He took my hand and led me to the hot tub. He slid into the water and held his hand out to help me in. I stepped in and sat beside him. I stretched my legs out and let the heat massage my body. He leaned forward and started rubbing my shoulders.

"What are we doing tomorrow?"

"Kayaking."

"I've never been kayaking."

"I will teach you."

The river glistened in the afternoon sun. The Georgia heat almost unbearable. Lee's height made that kayak look small. I kept paddling myself in a circle. Lee was chuckling as he instructed me on how to stop spinning. I attempted to shift and ended up in the freezing water.

When I surfaced, I was beside Lee? I pulled myself out of the freezing water and onto his kayak. I carefully climbed onto his lap, the waves rocking the kayak underneath us. I kissed his lips, then down his neck, my hands tangled in his hair. His left hand grabbed my butt and pulled me closer to him. The kayak rocked a little harder underneath our entangled bodies. The sun beating down on my back gave me a slight burning sensation. The oar slipped from his right hand and went to my bikini bottom. He untied the right side, then moved to the left. I reached into his shorts and grasped his long semi-hard penis. I wiggled his shorts down his waist a little, exposing it. I positioned myself over top of him so that the head was rubbing my clit with every bump in the water. Every bump made me want him right here, right now. My insides burned with desire. I looked into his blue eyes and saw my desire reflected. His shaft thickening and hardening with every touch.

He wrapped his arms around my body and cradled me against his chest. I felt his soft lips on the back of my neck as they caressed my skin. His hands wrapped around my waist, I traced the muscles across his chest and tenderly kissed my body. I slowly shifted my body. He thrust his penis into my wet pussy. He grabbed my hips and pulled me onto his hard cock. My pussy tightening with every pull and push. My eyes rolled back and my whole body quivered. His motions sped up, his body tensed up, until he blew his massive load inside my pussy.

Back at the cabin I was so exhausted that I could barely keep my eyes open to walk to bed. I changed out of my wet clothes and laid down. Lee wrapped up around me and I drifted to sleep.

The next morning, I woke up early. My hair felt slimy, so I grabbed a quick shower. I walked around the cabin. When I found what I was looking for I began cooking. The smell of bacon, sausage, and eggs filled the bedroom. Lee turned over and saw that I was gone. He laid his head back on the pillow and smiled. A few moments later I walked through the door. "Time to get up," I called. "Breakfast is ready."

"What is all this," he asked as he walked into the dining room. Bacon, sausage, eggs, toast, and a glass of milk sat in front of him. He sat down and started devouring his breakfast, meanwhile I sat there contemplating if I was going to tell Lee my secret. I owned the company he worked for. It was my name that got stamped on his weekly paycheck. This proposed a huge risk to them both. If the staff knew about this, he could lose his job. The press would make a headline out of this, and my integrity would be compromised. Every time they went out in public, I was at risk of being exposed. "Lee."

"Yes, darling?"

"I have something to tell you." I trailed off. Lee was watching me but still eating his breakfast. "I…" What if he does not love me? "I have a big surprise for you." I needed to know if Lee genuinely loved me before I told him my secret. I had never had a real relationship before. All my previous boyfriends wanted was my fortune. Guys like Lee always showed up to the staff Christmas parties with women who looked like dolls. Make up, high heels, nose job, skinny waist, afraid to eat any real food. Those type of women annoyed me. The kind of women who only wanted men like Lee for their money. For some unknown reason though those were the type of women men like him wanted. A tear ran down my cheek.

"Darling, are you alright?"

"Yeah." He walked across the room and wrapped me in his arms. He ran his hands through my hair. He knew this soothed me. I enjoyed his strong embrace for a few moments. The sound of his phone ringing startled them both. He left it ring and held me tight. When it rang again, he walked back the hallway and picked it up. "Babe, you done eating?" He stuck his hand out the door with a thumbs up. I cleared the table and was at the counter doing dishes when I felt his embrace again. "Everything alright?"

"Yeah, that was Greg making sure I'm coming back to work Monday."

13

"That man can't function without you, can he?"

"I don't think he can."

"In two weeks, I have to go to Tybee Island to meet my parents' lawyer. I was thinking maybe after we could go to the beach."

"I will have to see what work has planned. I signed up to go to California to help restore the power." My shoulders dropped; my voice lowered. My misery was extremely evident. "Or maybe I will stay. I will stay. Monday I will tell my supervisor that I can't go."

"No, if you want to go you should. I can't interfere with your job."

"If I am selected, I will visit. Are you selling your parents beach house?"

"I was going to, but I decided to keep it. The lawyer just needs me to sign off on the sale of the main house."

"How long has it been since they passed?"

"Ten years. I was nineteen when the police showed up. They called me into the Dean's office." The flashback was playing in my mind. My stare became blank. My words flowed from my mouth smooth a silk. "I went to a party that night and got alcohol poisoning. I went to the emergency room; my stomach was pumped and I flat lined. I saw my mom. She begged me to breath. I woke up surrounded by doctors and nurses, my lungs burned, and my stomach ached." His strong embrace pulled her back to reality. He wrapped his arms around me and lifted my chin, so I was looking for him in the eyes. Words exchanged with just looks. His desire to never see me suffer that much conveyed in his eyes.

He walked back the hall. I could hear his voice from the kitchen. "I can't go to California. I need the week of the tenth off. Thanks man." He walked back to the kitchen and into the dining room. He sat in a chair staring out the window.

"Is everything ok?"

"Yeah, I can go to Tybee with you in two weeks. I took the week off."

CHAPTER 4

MONDAY AFTERNOON I was on Newberry Hill with Becky. Lee was standing by the bucket truck with a stick. Greg shot me a look as he said, "Brother Smith get over here with your long hard stick."

"Are they seriously still trying to hook us up?"

"Yes." Becky grabbed my head and turned it towards the bucket truck.

"What?"

"Look at the ruler!" There on the tool comportment of the truck was a hand drawn ruler with the numbers eighteen, nineteen, twenty, and twenty-one. Under the number twenty was an arrow. Written directly below was the word, Lee. I turned and blushed. I did not tell Becky all the details about my weekend with Lee.

Becky and I returned home that evening and went to the swimming pool. We were enjoying the sun when I heard a familiar voice coming up the patio. "Sarah."

"What are you doing here?"

"Came to see you. Your neighbor said I could find you here. I woke him up knocking on your door." He sat on the chair beside me. Becky raised her eyebrows at me.

"I'm going to the store, Sarah, do you want anything?" We walked back to the apartment. Lee and I sat on the sofa until Becky left. I ran my hand down his chiseled chest. His body was tense. My fingers lingered over every inch of his toned abdominal muscles. As my hand traveled further south his body relaxed under my touch. I gazed into his eyes. Everything around me disappeared. My desire for him consumed my thoughts. He gazed back at me; our eyes locked until I realized he could see into my soul. I kissed his soft lips passionately. Lee grabbed my waist and pulled me onto his lap. He kissed my lips softly. His kisses grew feverishly enthusiastic. My hands entangled in his short brown hair. His kisses slowed and he pulled away for a second. I looked into his sparkling blue eyes. His gaze found mine and I got lost in his soul. I could see his unsaid thoughts, the pain and desire in his eyes.

He put his hands around me and pulled me closer, passionately kissing my lips and neck. His kisses on my neck intensified as he pulled my shirt up over my head. I found the button on his pants and started to undo them.

He turned and laid me on the couch. I started to slide his pants down his long legs. His phone vibrated on the floor. He ignored it and continued sucking on my hard nipples. The phone vibrated again. This time he stopped and picked it up. "I have to go."

"Is something wrong?"

"Someone hit a pole." He grabbed his pants off the floor and started putting them on. He handed me my shirt and put his boots on. We walked to the door; Becky was sitting on the couch watching television. When she saw us, her eyes turned? "I will call you." With a final kiss he walked down the sidewalk to his truck. When he reached the door he turned and looked back, I was standing in the doorway watching him. I watched as his truck disappeared then closed the door.

"What happened?"

"He got called to work."

"Did you guys hook up?"

"I don't kiss and tell." She returned to her television program. I walked to the kitchen and grabbed a snack then returned to the couch.

"I can't take it anymore. What happened?"

"We kissed."

"That's it?"

"Yeah, his work interrupted."

"That sucks. But better get used to that."

"It's fine." I finally looked at a clock and it read ten o'clock. I walked back to bed and laid down. I could not stop thinking about Lee. I wondered if he was ok but did not want to be clingy, so I did not message him. I woke to a knock on the door. I put my glasses on and walked to the living room. I opened the door and saw Lee standing there. "Lee, is everything ok?"

"Yes, darling. I just couldn't stay away." He walked in the door and stood there. I was blinking my eyes rapidly trying to wake up.

"What time is it?"

"Midnight, I didn't wake your roommate, did I?"

"She sleeps like a bear."

"Good. I have a surprise for you. I found something the other day and tonight is the perfect night to show you. Get dressed." I disappeared to my bedroom and dressed. We drove for what felt like miles until Lee turned onto a dirt road. He pulled into a parking lot and opened my door. "Hope you don't mind a little walking."

"Walking is fine." He took my hand and we walked down a gravel path. The moonlight that shone through the trees guided our way." We walked for a mile heading deeper into the woods as we went. He led me around a bend, behind the bend was a waterfall. In the clearing by the waterfall was a blanket and a small picnic illuminated by the moonlight. "This is so beautiful. How did you find this place?"

"I replaced a pole up that mountain." He gestured for me to sit down. "What brings you to Georgia?"

"My parents died a few years ago. They had a vacation house on Tybee Island. When they died, the entire estate was left to me. I met Becky and she told me about the job opening here. What brings you here?"

"I was stationed in Kingston at the time of my discharge from the Navy. I was an electrical engineer in the Navy and when I left, I jumped into electrical work. Signed into the union and traveled around since then."

"Thank you for your service." A slight breeze made me shiver. He took off his jacket and draped it over my shoulders, then pulled me in closer so we could cuddle and watch the waterfall. The light of the moon illuminated the water as it fell on the rocks below. I snuggled into his muscled chest. His strong arms caressed my body. My eyes grew heavy as he ran his hand through my wavy brunette hair. My eyes start to close, and I popped them open.

"Time to get you home darling." We walked back to the truck. I climbed into the middle and cuddled into Lee. My eyes grew heavy, and I could no longer stay awake. I woke up in my own bed with Lee beside me. I walked to the kitchen trying my best not to wake Lee. There was a note taped to the refrigerator.

"Sarah, went for drinks with Tim. Have fun, Becky." I grabbed a glass of milk and headed back to bed. Lee sprawled out over the bed. I stood in the doorway admiring how sexy he was. The ottoman at the foot of the bed told me that I needed a longer bed. His chiseled features made him look like a Greek God. Calluses on his hands reminded me that he worked hard. The teeth missing from his smile reminded me that he was human. His hands the size of a lion's paw, his boots at the bottom of the bed would have posed a tripping hazard for me. A smile danced across his face and melted my heart.

I walked to the living room and sat on the couch. When the sun started to rise, I walked out to the patio and called Alice. "Sierra, about time you answer my emails."

"Sorry, Alice been working long days."

"Do you have any data yet?"

"Have accounting run the numbers on a ten cent per hour pay raise for each flagger. What are the safety statistics on California power restoration?"

"Fifteen percent of the effected population is restored. The state assessed us a $100,000 fine for not upgrading our equipment. Five serious injuries last week, one fatality."

"What caused the fatality?"

"Defective equipment."

"Get all of our linemen new gloves, new fall harnesses, and a $300 boot allowance. Increase the number of our presence out there so that each person gets twelve on twelve off."

"What do you want me to order?"

"Have Liam choose three options of each form the catalog and email them to me."

"That puts six more of our guys in California. I will have to get Liam to call the union hall."

"Start implementing a bonus system for the flaggers and get a thirty-day meeting. Check how they are doing if they are happy."

"Ok. When are you coming back?"

"I want to get a few weeks in with the changes to see if things improve. Has our retention numbers gotten any better?"

"Still at seventy percent. So, what's this about a guy?"

"Who told you about that?"

"Chris has been in the office complaining about the new girl Sarah and a lineman. I told him that I would pass it along for a decision."

"I don't really know what we are."

"How do you not know where you stand?"

"It's complicated. He's so sexy though."

"Just be careful. Does he know who you really are?"

"No, I was going to tell him the other day, but I didn't."

"Good. Linemen are trouble. A lot of construction guys sleep around when they go out of town. Just make sure he's not married."

"He's going to Tybee Island with me so if you come with the attorney call me Sarah."

"You're taking him to you parents beach house? You must be serious about this guy. I will brief the lawyer." I put the phone on the table and laid my head on the table. The sound of footsteps on the patio made me sit straight up. I turned to see Becky smiling ear to ear.

"Where's Lee?"

"In bed." She walked over and sat down across from me.

"In your bed?"

"No in yours. Yes, my bed." She hit the table and howled. "What?"

"You hooked up."

"No." I blushed and a smile formed on my face.

"Good for you. Are you, his girlfriend?"

"I don't really know. We have not exactly labeled what we are yet. He's going to Tybee Island with me in two weeks."

"That's a big step for you. Even I haven't been to the beach house." I heard Lee's phone ringing in the bedroom. I ran in to grab it. I answered it and stepped outside of the room.

"Hello."

"Sarah, where is Lee?"

"He's sleeping. Do you need him?"

"He was supposed to help me fix my deck later. Just called to see what time he planned on coming."

"I'm going to cook him breakfast here shortly. When I wake him up, I will have him call you."

"Sounds good young lady. You have a good day."

"Thanks Greg. I will have him call you." Becky walked into the kitchen with a puzzled look on her face. "What?"

"You answered his phone. Definitely a couple." I started looking through the cabinets to see what we had for breakfast. "What are you cooking?"

"He needs protein." I was cooking bacon, eggs, and pancakes. Becky was staring at me.

"If all it took was a man in the house to get you to make a three-course breakfast, I would have got you a man a lot sooner." I threw her the dirty looks. "Burn a few pieces of bacon. I like mine burnt." I pulled most of the bacon off and left a piece in the pan cooking for Becky. Becky walked to her room, and I saw the email with approvals for the new equipment. I walked away from the stove to answer. I had just signed my name when the beeping of the smoke alarm reminded me that I had been cooking with grease. I ran over and took the pan off the stove. I tried fanning the smoke alarm. Becky and Lee came running into the kitchen.

I opened the patio doors, and the smoke alarm went silent. "Are you ok," asked Lee.

"Yes, Becky wanted burnt bacon and I guess it over cooked. "There's bacon on the counter. Eggs and pancakes too. Greg called."

"I forgot I am supposed to help him today. I will call him later." He grabbed breakfast and joined me on the patio.

"Tomorrow I have to leave for my parents place. If you need to stay and help Greg I understand."

"No, darling. I promised him that I would help him today."

"My parent's lawyer will be at the house Monday morning."

"We will be there by tomorrow evening." He sat his plate down and stood up. "I am headed to Greg's now. See you soon." He kissed my lips and walked to his truck.

CHAPTER 5

THE NEXT MORNING, I woke up and finished packing my suitcase. I walked out to the living room and saw Lee passed out on the couch. I approached Becky who was on the patio. "When did he get here?"

"Eleven-thirty last night."

"You could have woken me."

"He told me not too. Are you all packed?"

"Yes." I heard Lee's footsteps on the stone. "Good morning."

"Morning." He wrapped his arms around me and kissed my forehead. "What time do we leave?"

"Whenever you are ready. I finished packing this morning." We walked out the door and to Lee's truck. He grabbed his suitcase and followed me to my car. A few miles down the road Lee was asleep in the passenger seat. He stayed asleep until I stopped for gas.

"Go that way."

"Why?"

"There's a little farm down this road that has the best peaches." I followed his directions until we came to a farm. We stopped and bought a bushel of peaches. He watched as I took the first bite.

"Wow."

"I told you." He ate his peach and we chattered about random things

on the highway. When I pulled into the driveway of my parent's house
it was one in the afternoon. I grabbed my things and opened the door. I
ran upstairs to my parents' bedroom and got changed into my swimsuit.
I walked downstairs ready for the beach. "Up the stairs, last door on the
right."

I walked out to the kitchen and saw that Alice had the place stocked
up for my arrival. I was studying the food choices when Lee walked into
the kitchen. He wrapped his arms around me, and I turned. "Ready to
go to the beach?" Before he could answer I grabbed his hand and led him
out the door. I fired up the golf cart in the garage and drove it down to
the pier. I pulled into a space and grabbed my bag. I found a spot in the
sand for my towel, then rushed down to the water. I watched as the waves
crashed to the shore, leaving shells and creatures in their absence. The
sun was high in the sky, the beach was remarkably busy today.

"Hey," I screamed as chilly water splashed down my back. I turned
and saw Lee grinning. I splashed water back at him but missed. He
splashed me again. I splashed him again. People on the beach were
watching us. I noticed a fin in the water about one-hundred yards away.
I pointed to Lee, and he watched with me.

"It's a dolphin." I looked at him surprised that he made a fast
determination, "Dolphins swim beside Navy ships all the time. Shark
fins are more pointed." Behind that a group of fins surfaced. People
flooded the shoreline to watch as the dolphins got further out.

"I have never seen a pod before."

"I have a dozen times." I walked towards the boardwalk and looked
around for animals. I saw a jelly fish, a hermit crab, a starfish, and a
dozen sand dollars. I tossed the sand dollars and star fish back into the
ocean. Lee just watching me curiously.

"Every summer when we would come here, I would always toss the
sand dollars back into the ocean. My dad would say I was wasting my
time. I told him that I made a difference for one today and that's how

I would change the world. One person at a time." Lee smiled. He bent down, dug a sand dollar out of the sand, and tossed it into the water.

"When I first came to HJL they had a saying about random acts of kindness. I thought that it was just something they did for publicity, but I realized in my first year there that they believed in it. I helped in toy drives, food donations, and charity fundraisers. Mr. Summers believed in what he preached."

"That is good. It's nice to see a company stand up to what it says." I walked to my towel, then up to the golf cart. I drove back to the house and Lee started grilling steaks. We watched the sunset on the back porch. When it finally set, we walked inside and went up to bed.

The next morning, I climbed out of bed and made a cup of tea. While I was drinking my tea on the front porch Phil showed up. "Good morning."

"Morning, Phil." He sat down across from me and opened his briefcase.

"I know you have a visitor so do you want to discuss the personal matters first?"

"Yes." He pulled documents from his case and laid them on the table before me.

"Your parents mansion sold for four million dollars. This is the closing document that I need you to sign and here is the check. This has my fees and taxes already deducted." I signed the back of the title and looked at the check. "Here is the transferred deed for the beach house. Are you keeping the staff for the beach house?"

"Yes."

"There's one last matter of business to oversee. Your father's classic car collection has been sold, except for the 73 Corvette Stingray and the 74 Chevelle."

Lee walked out the door and sat beside me. I examined the bill of sale paperwork and signed the titles.

"I will submit this and the proper documents to their attorney. The checks I gave you can be deposited at your earliest convince." He took the papers and closed his briefcase. I shook his hand and he left.

"I didn't want to interrupt."

"You didn't. We were almost done anyway. He's not a social person." I slid the checks in my pocket so that Lee didn't see my real name. We walked to the kitchen and started cooking breakfast together. I mixed up pancakes while he fried the bacon. He sat me on the counter and kissed my lips. After breakfast we went for a walk on the beach. I collected seashells while Lee watched me. We sat on a swing and watched the waves crash to the shore as people filled the beach with their chairs, towels, and umbrellas.

"Did that lawyer say you have two classic cars coming?"

"Yes, my father had an extensive collection. All the cars sold except for two."

"That's cool."

"Yeah, the cars should be here before we leave."

"I am sure this is all hard for you. You don't have any siblings?"

"No, it is just me. My mother didn't have time for another baby. By the time I was in Kindergarten my father's career had taken off and my mother was too busy at the country club to be a mother."

"I am sorry to hear that."

Back at the house we were laying in bed watching television. I rubbed Lee's back then slowly kissed his neck. I pulled him down on the bed beside me and rolled on top. I pinned his wrists above his head, and he smiled. "Now, what you doing to do?" I slowly kissed my way down his perfect body, emphasizing every muscle. I kissed down his waist watching his reaction to my touch. The hunger in my eyes reflecting as I slowly got closer to his hard cock. I gently tickled his balls and let out a soft moan as I started kissing his hard penis. I licked up and down his hard shaft then down to his balls, pausing to watch him enjoy it. I felt his cock getting thicker. I looked into his eyes, "Fuck," he screamed as he exploded in a rush so powerful it almost choked me.

He pushed me down onto the bed and pried my legs open. His strong muscled arms wrapped around my thighs, holding me in place. He kissed my clit then slowly started licking mu pussy. "Oh," I moaned. He stroked my pussy in long, slow licks, all curling around my clit. "Fuck," I screamed as he pushed me to the point of squirting all over his face. He cleared his throat and pointed to the edge of the bed. He had a stern look on his face. I got up off the bed and walked to the edge. He pushed me forward until I was bent over, then he forcefully shoved his hard dick into my tight, wet pussy. He pounded my pussy, the length of his arousal almost brutal to endure. His movements didn't slow, the thrusts got harder and longer until I could feel his body get rigid as the pressure built. My pussy filled with warm cum as his grip tightened on my ass. He collapsed on the bed, his chest heaving and glistening with sweat.

Monday night we went out to eat. I had just sat down when I felt my phone vibrating in my pocket. I tried to ignore it, but it kept vibrating. "Excuse me for a minute. I walked to the restroom as my phone lit up again. "Yes, Alice?"

"Sierra, I need you to come back."

"I can't Alice. We are just getting to know each other."

"It's vital Sierra. The state of California has assessed us fees and you need to make a statement."

"Fine. I will be there." I returned to the table and sat down. Lee was just finishing a phone call as I sat down.

"Darling, I'm going to California for a while. I'm headed out on storm."

"I'm going to miss you. When do you leave?"

"Monday, I know that's only a week."

"I understand. Work is important and I will be here when you come back. We can talk on the phone while you're gone." The atmosphere around us fell silent.

"I'm so sorry sir but we are out of what you requested." I looked over and just then noticed our waiter standing there. Lee and I had been gazing at each other since we stopped talking.

"That's fine. We will just take the check then." The look on his face told me that we were thinking the same thing. Startled by the vibration of his phone against the table I jumped. "Darling, how about you head towards the truck. I will pay the bill and be along." I walked towards the door and stood there for a second, watching a young couple stumbling to get to their car. The woman looked around my age was so drunk that she stumbled right into the back of Lee's truck. I chuckled as he picked her up off the ground. Suddenly a strong set of arms wrapped around me. He led me to the passenger seat of his truck and opened my door.

We drove back to my parents' house. "What would you like to do first?"

I want to go swimming," I said as I reached into my bag and grabbed my bikini. I walked to the bathroom and turned on the light. "Are you coming," I asked as I walked into the bedroom as I was tying my top around my neck. He smiled and reached into his bag. I poked my head back in the bathroom and finished getting ready. "Can you grab," I walked out the door and turned straight to see his half naked body.

"Grab what," he asked as he caught me in his arms.

"My, my towel." He handed me my towel. I smiled up at him as I took the towel. I reached up and kissed his soft lips. We walked to the beach. I put my towel and shoes on the ground and stepped into the tide. I dove under the water. When I came back up, I looked at Lee standing on the shore watching me with a smile on his face.

"Are you coming in?"

"I'm admiring the view from here."

"I promise I will make it worth it." He put his towel and shoes with mine and got into the water. He swam over to me. "Race you to the prier," I said as I took off. I reached the pier and looked around for Lee. I did not see him, suddenly I felt strong arms around me. Lee picked me up and walked towards the shore.

I wrapped my arms around his neck as he walked with me. "I won't drop you," he said as I wrapped my arms around his neck. He leaned down and kissed my lips. I kissed him more passionately than I ever had before. We broke apart and gazed into each other's eyes. I could see all the pain in his eyes. I could see that he had been hurt before.

We walked back to the house, barely able to keep our hands off each other. He stood in the doorway watching me take off my bikini. "Are you coming," I asserted as I untied my bottoms. His eyes got big as he slowly walked towards me. He walked into the room as I untied my last string and let my bottoms fall to the floor. I kissed his lips and put my hands on his waist. I slid his shorts down his legs until they fell to the floor. I reached behind him and turned on the hot water. He kissed down my neck, while his hands slid down my back. His touch sent chills down my spine. I stepped into the shower and pulled him in behind me. I kissed his lips and started rubbing his penis.

"Mmmm," he moaned. His penis slowly got harder as I rubbed it. I got down on my knees and looked up at him. He was looking down at me watching me with every move. His hard shaft slid into my mouth. I twirled my tongue across the tip of his penis and slowly down the hard-long shaft. After a few minutes I stood up.

"Fuck me," I demanded. I bent over and he rubbed the head of his hard penis against my clit until I was wet. He slowly and gently slid his hard, long penis into my tight wet pussy. "Faster." He obeyed and went faster and deeper. "Good boy. Now make me squirt!"

He pulled out and pulled me up to face him. He kissed my lips and grabbed my legs. He picked me up and pinned me against the wall. He kissed down my neck and lavished my breasts with attention. His finger rubbed around a sweet spot and my eyes rolled back in my head. Every point in my body sparked with desire. It was too much to manage. He drove his finger inside me, setting off another scream of desire. He thrust another finger inside me, hitting the spot that turned my screams into a hot, sticky orgasm. He took his two fingers and shoved them in my mouth, forcing me to taste my own pussy. I licked my juices off his fingers as he pulled them out of my mouth. He put my feet back on solid ground then reached behind him and turned off the shower. He stepped out of the shower, handed me a towel, then walked into the room. I wrapped my towel around me and followed him into the room. I walked up in front of him and sat on the bed. He pulled my chin up towards him and locked eyes with me. I could see into his soul, his every desire becoming known. He laid down on the bed behind me. I curled up around him and laid my head on his bare chest. His heartbeat slowly soothed me to sleep.

The next morning, I woke up wrapped around Lee. I gently kissed his neck, then moved down his chest, emphasizing each kiss as I got lower. I pulled back the covers and untied his towel. I gently kissed his balls then up his shaft. As I slid the very tip of his penis into my mouth he stirred. "Good morning beautiful," he said as he looked down at me smiling. I continued to slowly move more of his growing penis into my mouth. "If you wanted breakfast, all you had to do was say so."

"Complaining?"

"Not at all," he said watching me go back to pleasing him. I continued sliding more of his hard cock into my mouth. I pushed myself to deep throat as much as I could manage then slid it out. I felt his body tense under my touch. I made one final push to deep throat as much as I could and he blew hot, sticky cum down my throat. I slid up so I was once again laying on his chest.

The alarm clock startled us both. I got up and started brushing my teeth. "We have a big day today," he announced.

"How so," I asked as I spit into the sink.

"You will see," he said smiling. He walked over and patted my forehead. We headed out for breakfast. "Eat up, you're going to need the energy." I filled my plate from the breakfast buffet and ate as much as I could. The whole time Lee gave me no hints about our activities today. After breakfast we drove to a field. The field had utility poles, tents, booths, and people everywhere. "Welcome to the Climbing Competition."

Before we walked into the event Lee grabbed climbing gear from the back of his truck. He walked over and reached into his bag. He placed a belt around my waist. "Almost but just to be sure we will stop by the tent and get you measured."

"Measured for what?"

"D-ring and belt size. We are climbing today as a team." I looked at the utility poles off in the distance. I realized that I had never told Lee about my fear of heights. He seemed so excited and proud when he said that we were climbing as a team that I knew telling him now would disappoint him. I walked over to the tent with him and got sized for climbing gear. After I was suited up and ready to go, we approached the practice poles. "I booked us a one-hour time slot to practice." He approached the judge in charge of keeping the practice time schedule. "Lee Smith, what time does my practice session start?"

"Elven to noon sir. The team climb starts at one-thirty. You are the last team to climb."

"Thank-you." He approached me. "Our training session starts in thirty minutes. I am going to grab us a drink. I will be right back." I looked up at the pole in front of me and gulped. Several groups of men walked by looking at me. The pole looked a lot taller up close than it had standing at the truck. Lee returned with bottles of water for us both. I drank my water, and the guy came over and handed me clipboard.

"Sign this please." I signed and handed the clipboard back.

"Excellent your time starts in five minutes. You have until noon to practice. No horseplay or your time will be cut immediately, and you cannot compete." I looked over at Lee while the man was talking. He looked so excited.

When it was our turn to climb, I followed Lee's instructions step by step. My legs burned as I started up the pole. Lee went first to demonstrate what I was to do. I reached the halfway point on the pole and decided to look down. Two dozen guys were standing below watching us climb. "Ignore them darling. Focus on my voice. You're doing great."

I looked up. Lee was to the top. I froze where I was, and my legs burned. Lee started down the pole towards me. "Sarah, are you ok?" Before I realized Lee was within reach. "Start moving down. Just like you came up but in reverse." I started to descend. "Great job, keep going." My feet touched the ground. Lee came down beside me. "Good job. Half-way your first time is excellent."

"But I didn't make it all the way."

"Darling, give it five minutes and we will try again." I massaged my leg muscles then stood up ready to get to the top this time. He started up the pole ahead of me again. I climbed halfway, my legs burning but I kept going. I kept my eyes on the pole in front of me and my mind on the next step. "Darling, be incredibly careful with your next reach. I'm right above you." I looked up and carefully placed myself, so my boot was right below Lee's. "Excellent." He leaned over and kissed me. "Now carefully head down."

"Are you guys ready to be timed?" Lee nodded. "You have thirty minutes left."

"Ok, darling. Same thing as last time but slightly faster."

"One at a time climb up, ring the bell, then climb down. Then the next person does the same thing. Time stops when the last person is on the ground. I recommend the newer climber goes first." I stepped up to the pole. "Ready." I nodded. "Go." I climbed up, rang the bell, and climbed back down. Lee did the same but in way less time. "Four minutes fifteen seconds." We practiced four more times each time slightly improving. "Next up."

We walked to the side and took the gear off. I looked around at the food choices. "What would you like to do?" Before I could answer my stomach growled. "Food it is then." We got food and found a place to sit. I watched the speed climbers practicing and was impressed. I ate half my burger then let it sit. Lee was devouring his food, oblivious to the fact that I was not eating anymore. I leaned over and nibbled on his ear. His body tensed at my advance. I kissed his neck. He stood up, checked the time, then pulled me to my feet. He pulled the doors open and stood me in the middle. "Bend over," he commanded. I bent over. "Pull your pants down." "Good girl," he said as I slid my pants down. He put his hand over my mouth and shoved his long hard cock into my pussy. He thrust his dick inside me deep and hard. I screamed with pleasure as he blew his massive load inside me.

"You will fuck me better when we go home tonight," I demanded. He smiled then grabbed his gear and headed towards the competition pole. We got over there just in time to catch the group before us start climbing. We came in third place in the competition.

When we arrived back at the house I went straight to the shower. When I got out there was a trail of pink rose petals on the floor. The smell of drakar filled the room. I followed the rose petals out to the hot tub. The area illuminated by the light of glowing candles, a tub full of rose petals, and a plate of chocolate covered strawberries was sitting on a table with a bottle of wine on ice. He reached down and pulled my tank top up over my head, then slid my shorts down my legs until they fell to the floor. He took my hand and helped me step into the tub.

I splashed him with water. "Hey," he said in a firm, demanding tone. He grabbed a towel and wiped the water off his face. He reached over and grabbed two strawberries off the counter. He handed me one and kept one. Our arms intertwined and I fed him my strawberry while he fed me his. "I forgot something." He grabbed two more strawberries and put some whipped cream on both strawberries. He fed me a strawberry covered in whipped cream then handed me a strawberry. I fed him the strawberry then climbed over him and kissed his lips.

He ran his hands down my shoulders. Enjoying the heat and the massage made me yawn. "Time for someone to go to sleep."

"I never knew pole climbing was so physically demanding."

"A lineman's work is hard work." I climbed out of the hot tub and grabbed a towel. I was putting on my pajamas when Lee walked into the room.

"You could have stayed in the hot tub." He pulled his shirt from the bed and tossed it to me. I put it on and climbed into bed. He curled up behind me and I went to sleep.

Wednesday morning, I woke up early. I was on the porch drinking my tea when the delivery truck arrived. "I have a delivery for Sierra Summers."

"That's me." I signed the ticket, and the man began unloading my father's cars. Lee came outside when I had the first car backed into the garage. The man handed me they key to the 73 Corvette, and I threw them to Lee. He caught the keys, and we went for a drive. His face lit up driving that car. We drove around for thirty minutes before he went back to my parents' house.

"Your father took good care of his vehicles."

"They were his pride and joy." I went upstairs and dressed for the day. We went on a drive up to Savanna. Lee showed me around the town pointing out the historic sites. Later that evening we returned to the house. While Lee cooked dinner, I took a shower.

When I was done, I put on see through white lingerie and put a Battleship Board on the table. When Lee came into the dining room, I was sitting on a chair placing my ships. He smiled as I gestured for him to sit down. He leaned in to kiss my lips. "No peaking," I demanded.

He grabbed his board and started placing his ships. I looked up with a smug grin, "Are you ready?"

"Just a second woman," he said with a determined look on his face. After a few moments he looked up, a serious but seductive look on his face. "Ladies first."

"J six."

"Miss. H three."

"Hit! I six."

"Hit. H four."

"Hit and sunk. I seven."

"Hit. A one."

"Hit. J ten."

"Miss. A two."

"Hit. An eight."

"Miss." His accent emphasizing the s sound. I looked up at him biting my lip, trying to hide my urge to tackle him. "A three."

"Hit. B seven."

"Hit. A four."

"You sunk my Battleship!" He crossed the bed. As he neared, I turned my board away from him. "No cheating." He took my in his arms and sat me on the table. He placed the boards on the seat where I had been sitting. My legs wrapped around his waist as I kissed his lips. His strong hand embraced my back while the other one grabbed my hair. I playfully bit his lip and whispered in his ear.

"Lead the way captain." He kissed down my neck. He slid his hand down my thigh sending chills up my spine. I kissed his lips passionately as my hands slid into his shorts and pulled out his cock. I pumped his shaft. His eyes showed me passion and desire. He wanted me; he needed my touch. He grabbed my hips and carried me up the stairs to the bedroom. He sat me gently down on the bed and stood in front of me. I dropped to my knees and slid his cock into my mouth. My tongue danced across the head vigorously. Inch by inch his cock went deep into my throat. I slid it back out to play with the head then slammed it deep into my throat. His body tensed as he exploded in my mouth.

I led him to the shower. Gray stone with a rain shower head, accented with black and white fixtures. He reached behind him and turned on the water. He placed my back against the cold stone, chills ran down my body. He slid me onto his massive rock-solid cock. He thrust deep into my pussy making me scream. His thrusts got faster. My screams got louder. His body tensed up as my pussy tightened around his pulsating cock. He exploded in my pussy as I scratched his back. "Lee," I gasped as I cradled into his chest. He stepped back so that the warm water bounced off our bodies. Our hearts raced as he cradled me in his arms.

CHAPTER 6

SATURDAY AFTERNOON I drove Lee to the airport. He wrapped his arms around me and kissed me. "Call me when you land," I told him. His flight got called to board. I gave him one last hug, then he turned and walked into the terminal. He stopped and looked back. I blew him a kiss. He smiled then disappeared. I waited until the plane was out of site then went to the car to grab my luggage. My flight left two hours after Lee's. I arrived in San Diego just in time to take Lee's call.

"Hey darling."

"Hey, how was your flight?"

"Boring. Did you make it home safe?"

"Yes."

"I just got settled into my hotel. The manager gave me the run down for tomorrow."

"You be safe out there."

"They said I can come back in two weeks."

"That's awesome baby. I can't wait to see you."

"I'm going to crash. Take care."

"Good night." I looked up as my luggage came off the carousel. Alice was there to obtain my luggage and guide me to a car waiting just outside for us. Once the driver put up the divider Alice opened her date book.

"Thursday morning you have a board meeting and Friday we have another press release to discuss the fines in California. All the major environmental groups will be present and asking lots of tough questions all geared at making us look like we don't care about the environment."

"Anything else?"

"Not at the moment." We arrived at Alice's apartment. I walked into her guest bedroom and sat my bag on the floor. Tomorrow was my first step back into the role of Chief Executive Officer. I laid down and woke up by Alice pounding on the door. "Sierra, get up. We got to leave for the conference soon."

I walked out the door five minutes later. Alice did my make up on the way there. "Sierra, you need to remember you're the CEO now. You need to worry more about your appearance." As we pulled up, the press surrounded the vehicle. "Ready?"

"Let's do this." She opened the door and cameras flashed everywhere. I stepped out and walked towards the podium. The lights were blinding. Alice approached the podium and motioned for everyone to settle down.

"Good morning, all. The purpose of today's conference is to address the environmental impact of Summer Enterprises."

I stepped up to the podium and faced the crowd. "Good morning, all and thank you for being here today. The recent fires have impacted thousands. Families and animals have lost their homes. Rescue and restoration workers injured, and some killed. Summer Enterprises will be planting one thousand trees and is ramping up it is restoration timeline on all equipment by fifty years. Additional safety equipment has been distributed to our workers in the field, labor numbers have increased to allow for shorter shifts and proper crews. Summer Enterprises accepts its responsibility for the damages and will further look for ways in which to aid the community it has damaged. Thank-you." I looked out at the silent crowd. "Any questions?" I stepped down and walked to the car. Alice stunned followed behind me. "That went well."

"I've never seen a silent press." We were at dinner when Lee called.

"Hello.," I said excited. Alice looked up at me above her menu.

"Hello darling. How was your day?"

"Boring. How was yours?"

"Good. I worked on pole 666 today."

"That's a bad omen."

"That's a bad omen because you aren't here." His voice changed. I smiled.

"I miss you too. Only thirteen more days." Alice was studying my face intently. The waiter came by to take her order and she motioned for him to go away.

"I'm almost back to my room. I will talk to you later." The phone cut out. Alice dropped her menu and the waiter reappeared. She gave him her order and turned to me.

"What happened?"

"I think he just realized he loves me."

"How?"

"His voice changed after he said he missed me. Then he rushed off the phone."

"How well do you know this man? Does he know who you really are?"

"We been dating all summer. No, but I took him to my parents beach house."

"Sierra, Phil said he's old enough to be your dad!" I took a sip of my drink and looked across the room. "Sierra!"

"It's my life Alice. I can do what I want."

"He's a lineman. Those guys are known for cheating. They go out of town and sleep around on their wives."

"He's divorced."

"Have you seen papers?"

"No, but I trust him."

"Honey, you've got no real relationship history. This man has been playing the game longer than you been alive."

"Why can't you just be happy for me?"

"I don't want to see you get hurt or worse. Extorted."

"Are you saying I'm not good enough for a man to actually love me?"

"Not at all sweethearts. I am saying you are not fake enough to be with a lineman. I know the type."

"Just because your ex-husband was a lineman and he cheated on you doesn't mean that's all of them!"

"You better check how you're talking to me young lady!"

"You're not my mother Alice. You're my assistant." She stormed out of the restaurant. I sat there picking at my food. The tables around me all watching me with a curious stare. I was about to leave when Greg called.

"Sarah, it's Greg. Lee is in the hospital. He got hurt on the job this evening."

"I thought he just got back not long ago."

"He did. They needed a couple volunteers to cover night shift and he volunteered."

"Is he ok? What happened?"

"He was up a pole working on a transformer and it exploded while he was climbing down. He has major burns. The doctors sedated him so he cannot feel the pain. He's also in a sterile room."

"Send me the address."

"It's ok. You do not have to come out here. I will keep you updated."

"Send me the address Greg. I there visiting restrictions?"

"Due to his condition there's no restrictions on visiting hours. When you get here let me know and I will go back with you."

"Thanks." I hung up and grabbed the nearest cab.

"Lee Smith please," I said to the nurse at the desk.

"Are you family?"

"I'm his girlfriend."

"Only immediate family is allowed in that room. I'm sorry miss."

"I'm Sierra Summers, CEO of Summer Enterprises and that's my boyfriend in that hospital bed. I demand to see him now!"

"Ok, let us not get hasty. He's in trauma room three."

"Thank-you." I headed towards the elevator and followed the signs up to the trauma center. When I got off the elevator, I saw Greg sleeping on the coach. I walked back the hall. As I got outside of room three, I heard a woman's voice. I rounded the corner and saw a woman sitting in the room with him. The press conference was on television behind the woman's head.

"Hun, this is Sierra Summers! She is here in your room! I can't believe it!"

"Is he awake?"

"No, he's still sedated. I talk to him like he is though. Doctors said he can hear me. If you need any information the rest of his crew is asleep in the waiting room. I'm Wendy, his fiancé."

"Nice to meet you. I just came by to check in." I walked out of the room as the tears streamed down my face. I rounded the corner to see Greg standing up.

"Sarah, what's wrong? Did he get worse?"

"No, he's fine. I met Wendy."

"Sarah, give him a chance to explain." Just then Wendy walked out and approached Greg. "I will tell Lee you stopped by when he wakes." Having understood Greg's words, I walked out of the hospital and down to the lobby.

I was sitting outside on a bench when my phone rang. "Sierra, where are you? The press is buzzing about you being at a hospital."

"It's a long story."

"Get out of there!" I flagged down a nearby cab and was on my way to a hotel when the news report came.

"Breaking news tonight folks. Summer Enterprises CEO Sierra spotted at a hospital just a few hours after she stunned the press by accepting fault for the fires. Sources say she went to the hospital demanding entry to a trauma room rumored to be occupied by one of her employees."

The driver turned down the radio, "That poor young woman, always being chased down by the media. No wonder she went into hiding. She's got her life to live yet."

"Yeah, she does. But people do not see things that way," I said as the tears started again. "I'm sorry."

"No need to apologize miss. You just came from the hospital no telling what news you got today." He handed me a tissue.

"I just found out my boyfriend has been lying to me. There was another woman this whole time."

"I'm sorry to hear that. Hopefully, things will get better."

"Thank-you." The rest of the trip went without words. I checked into a room, using my fake ID, and hoped for peace. My phone had been ringing off the hook. After the fifteenth call, I finally answered. "Yes, Alice?"

"Where are you?"

"I'm at a hotel under my fake ID."

"Which one? I am coming to get you. Send me the address." The phone went silent. I sent Alice my location and room number. I could not stop picturing the woman with Lee. Of course, I was not his choice. How could I be? Anger flooded my body. I was naïve to believe that we would be different and defy the odds. Felicia was right. Guys like him did not marry women like me. Besides, he now knew that I had been lying about who I was all summer. Was I wrong for wanting a man who loved me for who I was, not what I have?

A knock came at the door. I opened the door and saw Alice. "Sweetie," she said as she embraced me in a hug. I cried and Alice rubbed my back.

"You don't have to tell me until you're ready. Just let it out." Alice turned on the television. I screamed into a pillow as knock came on the door. Alice opened the door and saw Greg standing there.

"What do you want," she asked partially closing the door.

He grabbed the door and said, "To talk Miss Summers." She shushed him pulling him into the room and closing the door. "Lee doesn't know that you are Miss Summers. He still believes you are Sarah."

"That doesn't matter Greg. He lied to me all summer."

"He loves you. Give him a chance to make it right."

"You can't start a relationship with lies."

"Lee isn't the only one that lied now is he."

"I lied about my name so that people wouldn't realize I own the company. He lied about having another woman. How can you possibly speak for him?"

"He woke up this morning. He asked for you. Wendy was in the room when he said your name. She stormed out before he opened his eyes. Please talk to him." He walked out the door. I sunk down to the floor defeated.

CHAPTER 7

I T WAS THE night of the company party. Every year at the end of October Summer Enterprises threw a massive company party. Employees could bring their families, there was food and entertainment. I picked out a red silky dress and silver heels. Alice did my hair and makeup. She would have been an extraordinary mother but for some reason after her husband cheated on her she never remarried.

We climbed out of the limo and walked into the party. When time came, I approached the stage "Good evening, everyone. I want to thank all our staff for their arduous work and dedication this past year. A special thank-you to those who have helped with disaster restoration." Applause broke us across the crowd. When it died to silence, I continued. "Next year our commitment to safety will be doubling. All our workers and departments will be receiving updated safety equipment and enhanced safety training. We look forward to a better year and hope every one of you will be a part of our success. Without all of you I would not be here. Thank-you. Enjoy your night!" I stepped down and headed for the door.

I walked towards my room when a door opened and a voice said, "Hello beautiful." I stopped dead in my tracks. I knew that voice. That deep southern accent would never leave my head. I tried to ignore him, but the inability to function had already set in. I fumbled with the key until it slipped out of my hand and fell to the floor. I sighed. "You know you can't ignore me. Just the sound of my voice is making you lose control of your thoughts." His voice was getting closer as he spoke. I could feel chills down my spine. "That dress, wow!" I could feel the warmth of his breath on my neck. Chills radiated down my spine as he caressed my neck.

"Lee," I sighed trying not to give into his touch.

"Your heart is racing. Your thoughts jumbled. "The sound of my voice makes you want me." He stepped in front of me. A dozen yellow roses with red tips in his hand. He held the door open for me. He grabbed a cup of water and placed the roses on the counter.

"What are you doing here," I demanded.

"You know talking to me like that gets me hard."

"Shut up and answer the question."

"I need to make you angry more often."

"What are you doing here?" I was trying to stand my ground, but my insides burned with desire and my pussy was getting wetter by the second. He closed the gap between us and scooped me up. He carried me back to the bed and sat down. His kisses trailed down my neck and onto my breasts. He laid me on my back on the bed. He kissed his way down my body then slid my panties down with his teeth. He kissed the inside of my thick thighs and rested my ankles on his shoulders.

He kissed my clit then slowly started licking it. He thrust two fingers deep inside my tight, wet pussy. My back arched and my legs quivered. I screamed as I squirted all over his face.

"Be a good girl and get on your knees." He stood in front of me. I kissed down his jaw, down his neck, to his chest. I opened my mouth, and he shoved his hard dick in. He increased the pace and the length that was in my throat. I could feel pressure building as he neared climax. He pulled out and bent me over. He shoved his thick pulsating shaft into my dripping pussy. His grip like vices on my hips as he forced his penis into my pussy. The stretching of my insides hurt but was pleasurable. His grip tightened and his force increased. His body tensed and grew rigid. "Lee," I gasped as I bit his shoulder. His cock exploded and pulsated inside me.

I remembered the woman from the hospital. I thought about Lee loving her like he did me. Anger and jealousy raged in my mind. I straightened up and screamed "Get out!" I pushed him towards the door and slammed it as soon as he was out. I quickly turned the lock and sank to the floor.

"Baby, I'm sorry I lied. Please let me in and we can talk."

"Go away," I choked out through the tears. I walked to the bathroom and cleaned myself up. I found a little black dress that left little to the imagination and my favorite pair of heels. Once I was certain he was gone I left. I walked across the road to the bar and started downing drinks. I scanned the room making certain Lee did not follow me here.

"Can I buy you a drink," said a tall man as he approached me.

"Sure, I'm Sarah."

"Chance. A shot of jack and whatever the lady wants."

"Jack and coke." His face looked impressed by my drink choice. The bar tender returned with our drinks, and he sat down beside me.

He held his drink up and said, "Cheers to new beginnings."

"Cheers." I took a drink and winced at the burn. I forgot that bar tenders in the south had heavy pours. "How did you know I need a new beginning?"

"Everyone needs a new beginning. I come to this bar frequently and I've never saw you."

"I usually don't drink at all." My glass was empty, and my head was light. I paid my tab and stood up to walk and stumbled. He caught me in his arms.

"Let me walk you outside."

"I walked here."

"Let me walk you home. You can't even stand straight." He supported my weight easily. He towered over me by more than a foot. He walked me to the hotel. "Which room is yours?"

I handed him the room key as my head got foggy. The next morning, I woke up, my head pounding. There were clothes all over the room around me and a half naked man in bed beside me. I walked to the kitchen and tried to remember last night. As I made a cup of tea, I remembered something. We had sex. I sat on the couch and drank my tea.

"Good morning, beautiful," he said as he walked out interrupting my stare at the wall.

"What happened last night?"

"I enjoyed last night as you seemed to, however I am not that type of man. I would like to take you on a proper date next Saturday night." I looked at him in disbelief. "I'm serious."

"Sounds good. Just no more alcohol. I really shouldn't have drunk."

"Nope, a nice date." He was buttoning his shirt.

"You work for HJL?"

"Yes, I'm a lineman. Is that a problem?"

"No."

"Look no one is going to know about this. Just the two of us." He kissed my forehead and left. I sank down on the couch. What had I just done? Tears welled up in my eyes. I was almost sure I was not seeing him on Saturday. When I collected myself, I walked to the room and started cleaning up my clothes. On the night table was a note.

Sarah,

I enjoyed last night. I look forward to seeing you again.

Chance.

Below that was his number. I called Alice. "Sierra, how are you?"

"I'm ok."

"The press is getting closer to finding you. You need to come back."

"Book me a flight."

"Too risky. I'm going to have to come to you." I woke up with a sudden need to vomit. Hearing me vomiting Alice walked to the sink and held a wet washcloth on my forehead.

"What's wrong with me?"

"Food poisoning, stomach flu, nerves, pregnancy." Her voice turned snide on the last word.

"How did you-"

"I know you have a gentleman in your life. I saw the stuff in the drawer."

"We been dating for two months. I am seeing him again Friday night."

"I am going to go get you a test, you better figure out how to tell your boyfriend."

She returned with a brown paper bag in hand. I was sitting on the couch texting Chance when she threw the bag at me. "Hey!" Later that evening there was a knock on the door.

"Hey baby girl." He embraced me in a hug as he walked through the door. Alice turned her head from the television to Chance. He kissed my neck.

"Baby, I have company."

"Act like I'm not even here," said Alice as she turned back to the television. I led him back to the bedroom and closed the door.

"I don't know how to say this."

"You're pregnant."

"What? How did you know? I mean I don't know for sure."

"Baby, you're glowing. The smell of food makes you queasy. Your temper has been flaring up too." I slid the test out of the bag. "Let's find out together."

Waiting those two minutes for that test to be ready felt like ages. Finally, the timer was up. Chance looked first. "I'm going to be a daddy!"

He wrapped me in his arms and kissed my forehead. "We got to get you into a doctor. Daddy's little man needs medical care."

Alice unable to hide her feelings anymore burst through the door. "Did I hear baby?"

"Yes, Alice. Chance this is Alice. She's my best friend."

"Congratulations! I will call a doctor for you Sarah." Alice vanished to take care of calling a doctor. She returned moments later. "Monday at eight for ultrasound." Chance was so happy that I could not risk telling him who I really was. That night we went out with all of Chance's coworkers. He refused to drink since I could not and the guys all badgered him. It was hardly nine when I started feeling sleepy.

No sooner did I lay my head on Chance's shoulder I was out. I slept most of the weekend and Chance was all too willing to lay in bed with me and talk to my stomach. Monday morning, I drove to the doctor's office. I was filling out paperwork when the lady took us to an ultrasound room. She put this cold jelly on my stomach and soon a baby appeared on the screen. Chance pointed to the baby and said, "See I told you it's a boy."

"Actually, that's the cord. We will not be able to determine gender until twenty weeks or so. Which is not that far away. You're nine weeks pregnant right now."

"That means I got you pregnant the first night."

"That is possible. However, was there anyone within a week prior to that?"

"No." Chance was too excited there was no way I could tell him about Lee.

"Go ahead and clean up and we will get you in a room for a doctor." The doctor reported that baby looked healthy and set me up for another appointment. Chance was looking at the ultrasound pictures when I checked out.

After dropping me off Chance went to work. I called Lee. "Hello."

"Lee, its Sarah. I'm pregnant."

"Sarah, how far along are you?"

"Nine weeks." The phone went silent.

CHAPTER 8

WEEKS TURNED INTO months finally we had our anatomy scan. As we sat in the waiting room, we were both excited to find out what our baby was. The tech called my name. "Do you guys want to know what you are having?"

We both exchanged looks and said, "Yes." The tech started showing us body parts and finally got a clear look.

"It's a girl." I looked at Chance and he was smiling. He squeezed my hand.

On the way home he looked at me and said, "My mom wants to meet you. She's flying out in a couple weeks."

"That's cool. How about your dad?"

"He doesn't know yet. Him and my mom are divorced. I'm sure she will tell him after she meets you." He helped me into the house and started cooking diner. Later that evening his phone rang. "I told her you're coming mom. You will love Sierra. It's a girl. We haven't picked a name yet." He hung up and walked into the room. "Baby what do you think of the name Georgia?"

"I like it. Georgia Leeann?"

"That's beautiful."

"Leeann was my mother's name."

"I wish your parents were here to meet her."

"Me too. I have a house in Georgia. It's a three bedroom so we would have room for a nursery."

"I can ask work to transfer me back to Georgia. I will ask Liam on Monday."

It was the middle of the night when I woke. I walked to the restroom. On my way back to bed I felt a gush of water. "Chance." A sharp pain shot through my stomach. The light turned on and Chance came running. "It's time." Chance walked me down to the car. He called work while he drove towards the hospital. I called the doctor.

"It's likely your water broke. Come into the hospital and we will check you out."

"What did the doctor say?"

"Said go to the hospital." The contractors started. I screamed.

"Breathe in and out sweetie." I started breathing. We arrived at the hospital. Chance pulled up front a nurse helped me into a wheelchair while he parked the car. When Chance came inside, they escorted us to labor and delivery. I wasn't on the monitors long before the doctor walked in and checked my cervix.

"Eight, negative two and moving. It's time to have a baby." I looked at Chance afraid of the pain I was about to endure. He squeezed my hand and rubbed my back. "It's time to push. Stop when you feel the ring of fire." I pushed until I felt a burning sensation. I gave the largest and hardest push I could, and I heard a baby cry. "It's a girl." Chance cut the cord and they placed Georgia on my chest. After an hour the nurse came and took Georgia to get cleaned up.

Later that evening while Chance was sleeping, I asked the nurse about a paternity test. "I can call the man and he can come take the test. We don't have to tell this young man if you don't want us too." I pulled Lee's number from my phone and wrote it down for the nurse. "I will give him a call and see what he says."

The second day in the hospital Chance had to meet his boss to get paperwork for paternity leave. He left the room. The nurse approached me and said, "We are just waiting for Mr. Smith to show up for his paternity test.

"Were you able to contact him?"

"Yes, I called him yesterday and he said he would be in sometime today."

"Does he have to come to this room?"

"No, he can take the test at the nurse's station. I know that we are to keep it confidential from the young man in the room. I will make my replacement aware and leave a note at the desk if he isn't here before I leave." Another nurse brought Georgia in for me. I picked her up and snuggled her. Just then Chance rounded the corner.

"Hey, baby my dad is here. He came to meet Georgia."

"Baby, that's great. Let me finish feeding her, and he can come in." He walked out of the room and back in. "He's going to wait in the waiting room. I just have to go get him when we are ready."

Chance helped me finish feeding the baby. Then he rushed out of the room to get his dad. "Baby, this is my dad, Lee." I tried to hide the fact that I knew Lee. Chance was too busy handing Georgia to Lee to realize that I was bad at hiding my expressions. Lee held Georgia in his arms and Chance beamed.

"Son, she's beautiful." He handed Georgia back to Chance and stood up. "I must be going."

"But dad you just got here."

"Son, I have to get back to work."

"Dad." Sally walked into the room. Lee walked out.

Printed in the United States
by Baker & Taylor Publisher Services